~FIRST GREEK MYTHS~
PERSEUS AND THE MONSTROUS MEDUSA

BY SAVIOUR PIROTTA
ILLUSTRATED BY JAN LEWIS

ORCHARD BOOKS

~ CAST LIST ~

PERSEUS
(Purr-see-us)

MEDUSA
(me-duce-a)

A monstrous
creature

FIRST GREEK MYTHS

PERSEUS AND THE MONSTROUS MEDUSA

For Jake and Fleur Pirotta
S.P.

To my boys
J.L.

WORCESTERSHIRE COUNTY COUNCIL	
090	
Bertrams	15.04.06
JEe	£4.99
RE	

Serie_ _reading con_____ _Prue Goodwin,_ lecturer in
Lit_____ _in Education at the University of_ Reading

ORCHARD BOOKS
96 Leonard Street, London EC2A 4XD
Orchard Books Australia
32/45-51 Huntley Street, Alexandria, NSW 2015
This text was first published in Great Britain
in the form of a gift collection called *First Greek Myths*, in 2003
This edition first published in hardback in Great Britain in 2005
First paperback publication in 2006
Text © Saviour Pirotta 2005
Cover illustrations © Jan Lewis 2003
Inside illustrations © Jan Lewis 2005
The rights of Saviour Pirotta to be identified as the author and
of Jan Lewis to be identified as the illustrator of this work
have been asserted by them in accordance with the
Copyright, Designs and Patents Act, 1988.
A CIP catalogue record for this book is available from the British Library.
ISBN 1 84362 808 2 (hardback)
ISBN 1 84362 786 8 (paperback)
1 3 5 7 9 10 8 6 4 2 (hardback)
1 3 5 7 9 10 8 6 4 2 (paperback)
Printed in China
www.wattspublishing.co.uk

There was once a young man called Perseus whose mother was very beautiful.

His father had died when he was a baby, so Perseus and his mother were all alone in the world.

The evil king of the land was desperate to marry Perseus's mother. But every time he asked her, she said no. She did not like his angry, mean face.

Perseus did his best to protect
his mother from the king's anger.

So the evil king planned to get rid
of Perseus.

One day the king called Perseus to his court. "I will leave your mother in peace," he said, "but only on one condition...

"You must bring me the head of the monster Medusa on a plate."

"Your wish is my command," said Perseus, trying not to tremble, and off he stamped.

Medusa and her sisters were
scary monsters called Gorgons.
Instead of hair, they had snakes
sprouting out of their heads.

Anyone who looked at Medusa's
face was instantly turned to stone!

Perseus knew he would need help to defeat her. So he went to see a wise man.

"I have promised to take the king the head of Medusa on a plate," Perseus told him.

"You are a silly boy," gasped
the wise man.

But he gave Perseus a shield. It
was so shiny that Perseus could
see his own reflection in it.

"When you kill the Gorgon," the wise man said, "do not look directly at her. Use this as a mirror."

Then he handed Perseus a sword with a crystal blade, strong enough to cut off Medusa's head.

Finally, he said, "Medusa is a very dangerous monster. You will also need... a helmet that will make you invisible,

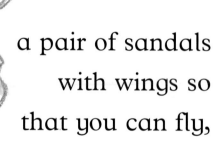

a pair of sandals with wings so that you can fly,

and a silver bag to put her head in."

14

"Where will I find them?" asked
Perseus.

"Go and see the three witches
who live at the bottom of Mount
Atlas. They only have one eye
between them, so it should not be
difficult to creep up on them."

Perseus thanked his friend and set off.

"I hear footsteps," said one of the witches as Perseus approached.

Her sister took the eye.

"I can't see anything," she said.

"Let me have a look," whined the other sister.

But just as the second witch was handing over the eye, Perseus leaped forward and grabbed it from her hand.

"No need to snatch," cried
the witch, thinking it was one
of her sisters.

"It wasn't me," said the
first witch.

"Then who was it?" the three
witches cried together.

"Me!" shouted Perseus boldly.
"And I will only hand it back if
you give me what I want."

"What do you want?" they demanded, all three together.

"Sandals with wings, a magic helmet and a silver bag. I know you have them," answered Perseus.

The witches knew they had no choice. They gave Perseus what he wanted.

Now the young hero had
everything he needed to kill
Medusa. He gave the witches back
their eye and headed for the
Gorgons' lair in his winged sandals.

As he flew through the sky,
Perseus felt scared. But he knew
he had to be brave and save his
mother from the evil king once
and for all.

He put on the helmet to make himself invisible and flew into the Gorgons' cave. He had never seen such a terrible sight.

The snakes on Medusa's head were hissing loudly. Her sisters wailed noisily on either side of her.

Perseus drew his crystal sword
and dived at Medusa. She heard
him coming and looked up.

The snakes hissed louder and her sisters screamed. How had someone got into their cave without them noticing?

Perseus grabbed a handful of
Medusa's snakes and, using his
shield as a mirror, he raised
his sword.

With one blow, Medusa's head
flew off her neck. Quickly, Perseus
put the head in his silver bag and
swooped up into the air.

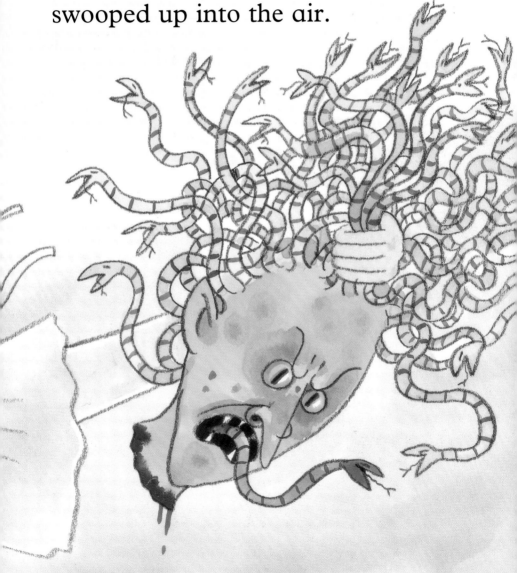

Medusa's sisters chased after him. Though they could not see him, they could follow the smell of Medusa's blood.

But they could not keep up with Perseus in his winged sandals.

As soon as he was home, Perseus went straight to the evil king. The king was surprised to see him alive.

Have you brought me what I want?" he asked, smiling to himself. "Ha! Of course you haven't. Now I will marry your mother after all."

But Perseus suddenly pulled
Medusa's head out of the silver
bag for the cruel king to see.
"Do you like it?" he asked.

Of course, the king did not reply. He had looked at the face of Medusa and was turned instantly to stone!

~FIRST GREEK MYTHS~

BY SAVIOUR PIROTTA ~ ILLUSTRATED BY JAN LEWIS

- ❏ King Midas's Goldfingers   184362 782 5   £4.99
- ❏ Arachne, the Spider Woman   1 84362 780 9   £4.99
- ❏ The Secret of Pandora's Box   1 84362 781 7   £4.99
- ❏ Perseus and the Monstrous Medusa   1 84362 786 8   £4.99
- ❏ Icarus, the Boy Who Could Fly   1 84362 785 X   £4.99
- ❏ Odysseus and the Wooden Horse   1 84362 783 3   £4.99

And enjoy a little magic with these First Fairy Tales
By Margaret Mayo - illustrated by Philip Norman

- ❏ Cinderella   1 84121 150 8   £3.99
- ❏ Hansel and Gretel   1 84121 148 6   £3.99
- ❏ Jack and the Beanstalk   1 84121 146 X   £3.99
- ❏ Sleeping Beauty   1 84121 144 3   £3.99
- ❏ Rumpelstiltskin   1 84121 152 4   £3.99
- ❏ Snow White   1 84121 154 0   £3.99
- ❏ The Frog Prince   1 84362 457 5   £3.99
- ❏ Puss in Boots   1 84362 454 0   £3.99

First Greek Myths and First Fairy Tales are available from all
good bookshops, or can be ordered direct from the publisher:
Orchard Books, PO BOX 29, Douglas IM99 1BQ
Credit card orders please telephone 01624 836000
or fax 01624 837033
or e-mail: bookshop@enterprise.net for details.

To order please quote title, author and ISBN
and your full name and address.
Cheques and postal orders should be
made payable to 'Bookpost plc'.
Postage and packing is FREE within the UK
(overseas customers should add £1.00 per book).

Prices and availability are subject to change.